Hospitals Aren't So Scary

by
Heidi Walters

AuthorHouse™
1663 Liberty Drive
Bloomington, IN 47403
www.authorhouse.com
Phone: 1-800-839-8640

First published by AuthorHouse 2/17/2010

ISBN: 978-1-4490-7163-9 (sc)

Library of Congress Control Number: 2010901228

Printed in the United States of America
Bloomington, Indiana

This book is printed on acid-free paper.

authorHOUSE®

It was a sunny Saturday morning, and Timmy had decided to go for a bike ride. Riding his bike was one of his favorite things to do. Timmy was riding on the road, and he could feel the warm sunshine on his face and the wind blowing in his hair. He was also thinking about what he was going to do after he was done riding his bike. Saturday was his day to do whatever he wanted. Timmy now was coming up to his driveway. He started to turn into the driveway but didn't realize that he was going too fast, so when he put his brakes on his bike, he slid sideways and hit the ground, his bike landing on top of him. He started to cry. Timmy's mom came running out of the house to see if he was all right. She said, "Timmy, did you get hurt?"

Timmy said, "Yes, my elbow hurts."

His mother said, "We'd better go to the hospital and see what is wrong with your elbow."

When Timmy and his mom arrived at the hospital, nurse Nancy met them by the door. Nurse Nancy saw that Timmy was crying, so she took him to a room to wait in while the doctor talked to his mom.

Timmy was sitting in bed when he heard someone say, "Hi, Timmy, my name is Brad the Bed." Timmy was surprised to hear a voice coming from a bed but he wasn't scared. Brad the Bed continued, "Timmy, look at the buttons on my side rails. One button is for the TV on the wall. You can watch TV whenever you want. Another button is for calling nurse Nancy if you want something to eat. And if you have a question for the nurse, you can push the button, and she will come to your room right away. See, Timmy, the hospital isn't so scary," concluded Brad the Bed.

3

Then, nurse Nancy entered the room and said, "Timmy, I have to take your blood pressure."

Timmy then heard a voice say, "Hi, Timmy, my name is Sarah the Stethoscope. The nurse will put your arm in a cuff that is hooked to the rubber tubing, which leads to a rubber ball. The nurse will squeeze the ball, and the cuff will get tighter on your arm. This won't hurt. It just feels like it's hugging your arm. I will listen for your heartbeat—boom, boom, boom. I hear your heartbeat, Timmy. Nurse Nancy will let some air out of the cuff now—shhhhh, shhhhh. Now, I am finished taking your blood pressure."

"Your blood pressure is good," said nurse Nancy.

Timmy said, "That didn't hurt at all, and I was not scared, either."

Next, nurse Nancy wanted to take Timmy's temperature. Timmy was then introduced to Thelma the Thermometer. Thelma said, "I won't hurt you. The nurse will just put the pointed end into your ear and press a button, and then you will hear a beep." A few minutes went, by then it sounded—beep, beep, beep. Then, Timmy knew that Thelma was done taking his temperature.

Nurse Nancy said, "Timmy, your temperature is good.

Thelma the Thermometer said, "That wasn't too scary, was it, Timmy?

"No," Timmy replied, "I wasn't scared at all."

The next stop was the X-ray room. Timmy sat in the chair by the X-ray machine that said, "Timmy, I'm Ray the X-ray Machine. I won't hurt you. Just put your arm on this metal plate. It might be a little cold. Now, the nurse will go in the other room and push a button—beep. There, Timmy, I just took a picture of your arm."

Dr. Dan came in the room and looked at the X-rays and said, "Well, Timmy, good news. There are no broken bones. Now, we will go back to your room where Brad the Bed is."

"Bye, Timmy," said Ray the X-ray Machine.

Timmy replied, "That didn't hurt at all. Thank you for being so nice to me."

Timmy and nurse Nancy arrived at the room where Brad the Bed was. Timmy immediately sat down on Brad the Bed. Nurse Nancy went out of the room and she retuned with Bill the Pill for Timmy to take. "Hi Timmy, How are you doing?" Bill asked Timmy. Timmy replied, "My arm hurts." Bill the Pill said to him, "Don't worry Timmy I'll help take some of your pain away. There are different ways that you can take me. One way is to swallow me whole, or I can be crushed up and put into applesauce. Sometimes you can even chew pills too. I come in many different shapes and colors, so don't ever mistake me for candy, because you can get sick if you take too much of me."

Nurse Nancy gave Timmy a blue pill and he decided to swallow it whole. Timmy said to nurse Nancy, "That wasn't scary, I'm happy to know there are different ways that you can take pills."

Dr. Dan wanted Timmy to have a shot. A shot is a needle with medicine inside it. Shots also help pain go away. Nurse Nancy brought in a needle with some medicine. A voice then said, "Hi, Timmy, I'm Nellie the Needle. Dr. Dan wants you to have me, too. When Bill the Pill can't handle all the pain you have, then it's my turn to help get the job done." Nellie the Needle continued, "Some people are scared of me. I feel sad that so many people don't like me. All that happens is that I give you a little poke and then the doctor pushes on the top of me. The medicine will go into your arm, and it will help your arm feel better."

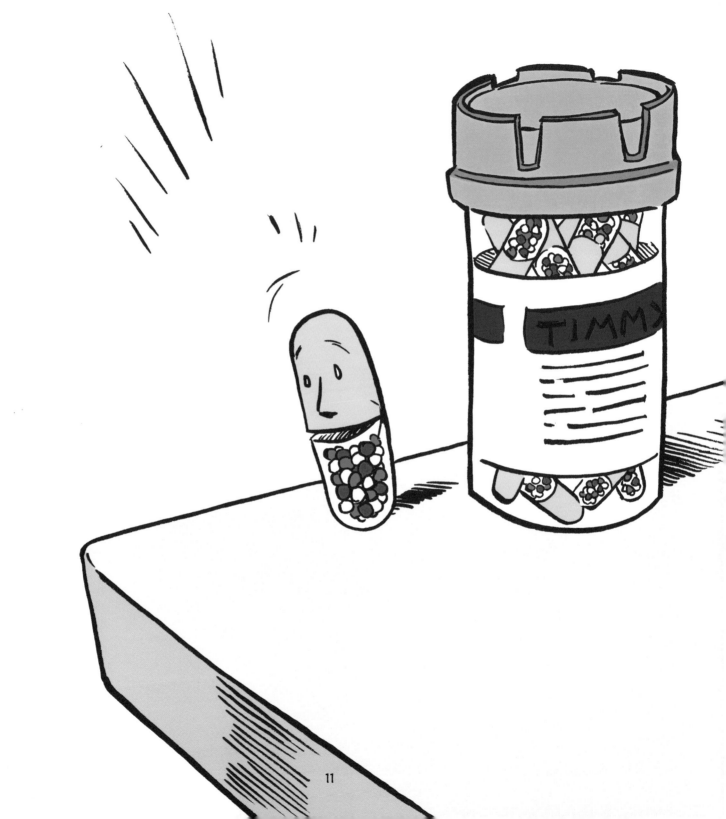

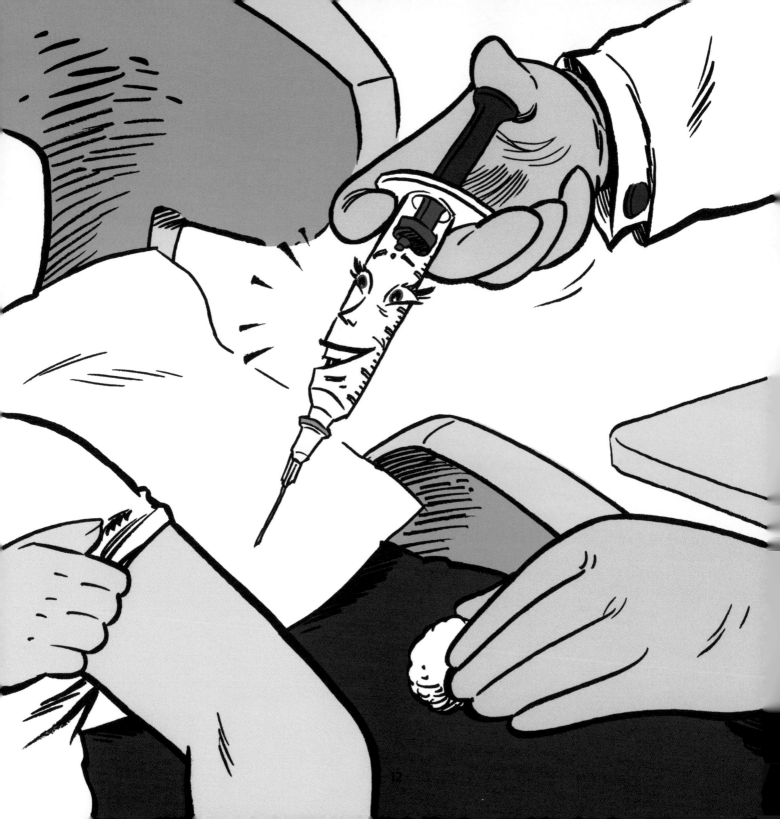

Dr. Dan put the needle in Timmy's arm. Timmy was a little scared, but after a quick poke from Nellie the Needle, the whole shot was done. Timmy said to Nellie the Needle, "That wasn't so bad. It hurt just a little bit.

Nellie the Needle said, "I'm happy I didn't hurt you, Timmy. I hope your arm is feeling better. You be careful riding your bike from now on, okay? I don't want you to hurt yourself again."

Dr. Dan said, "The X-ray doesn't show anything wrong with your arm or your elbow. You might just feel a little sore from falling on it. I'm sure you will feel better in a few days. You can go home now."

Timmy said "Thank you Dr. Dan for helping me today."

Dr. Dan replied, "I'm happy that your arm is going to be okay. Good-bye Timmy I'll see you later."

Nurse Nancy explained to Timmy how Ray the X-ray Machine, Thelma the Thermometer, Sarah the Stethoscope, Bill the Pill, and even Nellie the Needle all had to work together so that the doctor could see what was wrong with Timmy's arm. "That is what we call teamwork. If everybody helps out a little bit, a big job can be accomplished. See, Timmy, the hospital isn't so scary after all."

Timmy smiled and looked at all the friends that had helped him feel better: Brad the Bed, Bill the Pill, Ray the X-ray Machine, Thelma the Thermometer, Sarah the Stethoscope, Nancy the nurse, Dan the doctor, and even Nellie the Needle.

Before Timmy left the hospital, Laura, the receptionist, gave Timmy a lolli-pop. Timmy said, "Thank you for making my arm feel better," and waved with his other arm good-bye to everyone. Timmy got in the car with his mom. As they were driving home,

Timmy said, "Mom, the hospital isn't so scary after all. I'm happy that you took me there. Now we know there is nothing wrong with my elbow."

Timmy's mom replied, "I'm happy you feel that way, Timmy. Hospitals are there to help people get better. That's why I decided to take you there. Timmy, now we know your elbow is going to be okay."

When Timmy and his mom arrived back home, Timmy's mom smiled at him. She was happy that she made the decision to take Timmy to the hospital.

LaVergne, TN USA
18 March 2010
176489LV00004B